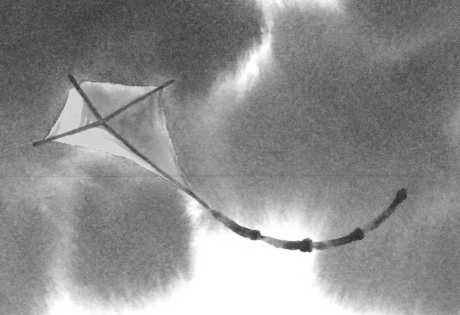

Alan C. Elliott

ON SUNDAY
THE WIND CAME

illustrated by Susan Bonners

William Morrow and Company   New York 1980

Library of Congress Cataloging in Publication Data

Elliott, Alan C
   On Sunday the wind came.

   Summary: A young boy describes the weather on each day of the week in terms of
the activities possible for him and his friends.
[1. Weather—Fiction. 2. Play—Fiction] 1. Bonners, Susan. II. Title.
PZ7.E434On   [E]   79-19083
ISBN 0-688-22218-8   ISBN 0-688-32218-2 lib. bdg.

Printed in the United States of America.
1 2 3 4 5 6 7 8 9 10

For
Christopher
Elizabeth
John
Laura
Lisa
Marcie
Peter
Thomas
Valerie

On Sunday the wind came from the east.
It whistled through the trees,
and when I raked the leaves in my yard,
the wind blew them up into the air.

Kites flew in the wind at the park.
The sky was covered with
big-eyed monsters,
long-tailed dragons,
and pretty butterflies.

Way above the kites,
the wind blew the clouds.
High clouds,
tall clouds,
dark clouds.
What will the weather bring?

On Monday the dark clouds
brought the rain.
When the clouds
bumped into each other,
lightning flashed,
and thunder roared,
and the rain poured.

I put on my raincoat and my big black boots.
My friends and I
found a stream
going down a hill
in my backyard,

and we raced twig boats
and paper boats,
and leaf boats in the water.
I held out my tongue to taste the fresh rain.
What will the weather bring next?

On Tuesday a curtain of fog hid the whole world.
It covered the houses on my street,
the trees in the yards,
and even my two cats.

The lights from the cars going down my street
glowed in the fog like big yellow eyes.

My friends and I played
hide-and-seek in the fog.
"Catch me if you can!" I said.
Every place was a place to hide.

When I breathed on my window, it fogged over,
and I drew happy faces and sad faces,
and one face that looked just like me.

I stayed inside where it was dry and warm.
My cats snuggled up to the fireplace,
and so did I.
What will happen now that the weather is so cold?

On Thursday the sleet came.
Cold little drops of water and ice
coated everything.
Icicles hung from the roof,
and the trees bent down low.

When everything was frozen,
my friends and I made sleds
of boxes and an old piece of tin.

Then we
   slid
      down
         the hill
            behind my house.

What more could the weather bring?

On Friday the sky was filled with
new white snow.
Flakes of every shape
swirled in the air
and covered the ground
like a blanket.

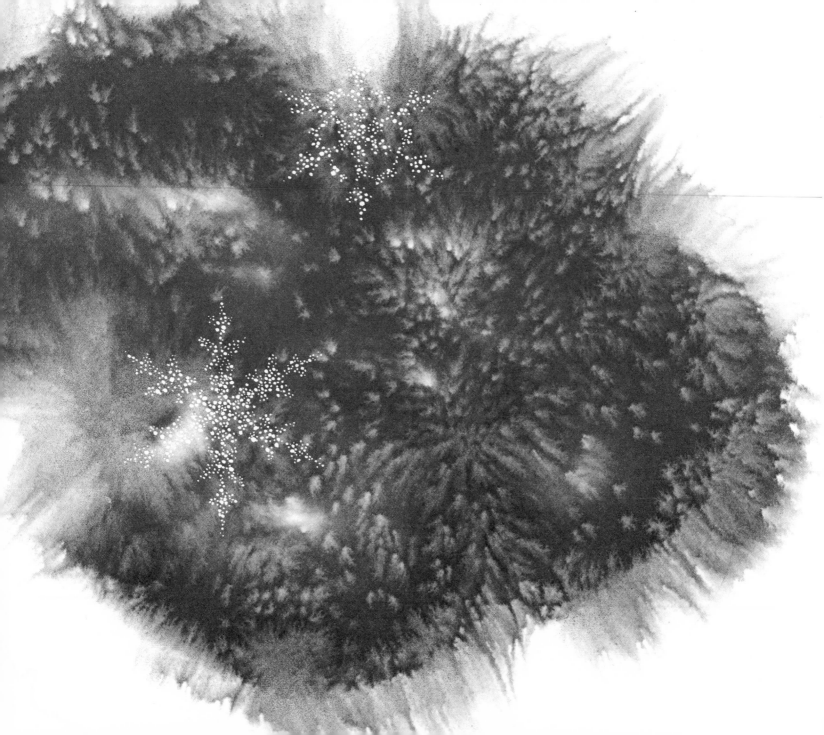

I put on my mittens,
my hat,
and my snug brown coat.
Then my friends and I made
a snowdad, a snowmom,
and two snow kids.

We made snow angels on the hill,
and we built a snow fort and threw snowballs.

Splat! Right in the face!

When a new wind came from the south,
and the clouds started rolling away,
I knew the snow would not last long.

On Saturday I saw the sun.
Its bright yellow face
warmed up the cold,
melted all the snow,
and dried up all the wet.

I put away my raincoat and my big black boots.
I put away my mittens and my hat,
and I hung my snug brown coat in my closet.

Then I ran into the bright warm sun,
and I gathered all my friends together,

and we played,